I0520382

ROGUE BEAUTY

AN EVE OF LIGHT SHORT STORY

HARAMBEE K. GREY-SUN

HYPERVERSE BOOKS, LLC

ALSO BY HARAMBEE K. GREY-SUN

Standalone Stories

Beholder

Love Among the Ultramoderns

The *EVE OF LIGHT* Series

The Novels

BloodLight: The Apocalypse of Robert Goldner (*Prequel*)

Broken Angels (*Book I*)

Divinities, Entangled (*Book II*)

The Short Stories

FoolKillers

The Lark

Heaven's Gun

Knotty & Ice

Rogue Beauty

Deviant-Hunter's Sabbath

BY HARAMBEE GREY-SUN

Poetry

Spring's Fall (Autumn Numbers * Book I)

Wine Songs, Vinegar Verses

Published by **HyperVerse Books, LLC**

www.hyperversebooks.com

writing between and beyond the lines

ROGUE BEAUTY

It's easy to kill ugly things.

The urge wells up like sexual desire, easing through the body, imbuing the soul as it pushes back against the disgusting assault on the senses. Only the repressed, the *normals*—the plain Janes and Johns—successfully suppress what their bodies are telling them to do. Yes, there are lines—but to the wise, those lines are blurry.

Only a despicable character would pass by a well-maintained flower garden and have a sudden urge to trample everything in sight. But consider a pretty girl of stable disposition passing by the front yard of a careless homeowner, one who has let weeds overtake the grounds to such an extent it appears to be a tallgrass prairie. Since the environment is clearly a reflection of the one charged with maintaining it, it would be easy to understand and excuse her taking a scythe to both owner and his property.

Only the most twisted among us would ever consider decapitating a puppy or putting a kitten in a blender. But if a sympathetic gal observed a wheelchair-confined boy with a stumped appendage and at least one other physical deformity, a boy prone to incessant drooling and spontaneous fits and violent outbursts, verbal and otherwise, she'd rightfully wonder how his parents could be so inhumane as to allow him to suffer incessantly and how society could allow the parents to let the boy live a life of unending misery and, while she wondered, her subconscious would nudge her into the role of merciful angel, a role the plain Janes and Johns would misinterpret as villainous.

Then there were the more complicated scenarios, those involving truly vile creatures, all aided and abetted by the Janes and Johns. This is where the lines surpassed blurry and twisted into wavering spirals. There were dimensions to true justice, shades to beauty...

My sunrise exercise could give me quite a charge.

I ran through a rumination of colorful scenarios and contrasts every morning while applying my makeup, and the runner's high sometimes became so overwhelming I inadvertently squeezed a steel canister out of shape.

My makeup came in reinforced containers, specially made. The powders and paints themselves had been specially formulated, concocted by doctors and scientists who'd devoted their careers to studying the White Fire Virus and devising ways to keep its carriers comfortable. The hope, perhaps, was that if the carriers felt comfortable enough, moral enough, *pretty* enough, they'd be more inclined to do whatever they could to tamp down their strange urges and not display the supernatural abilities that neither they nor the doctors nor the scientists truly understood. The same pharmaceutical company that sold the makeup also produced the prescription-only lotion I applied to my hands and forearms, my ankles and calves, and—on the days I was so inclined to wear an outfit that would leave it exposed to light—my midriff.

My authorized prescriptions had run out some time ago. But I had good connections. One of them stood in the bathroom's doorway, watching me, waiting for the day's agenda.

"Yesterday: whore chic," Bruce said. "Today: businesswoman bleak?"

"Necessary," I said as I applied eyeliner. "I need to charm my way through an office building, not a Marriott. Today's target is an old colleague."

"Yeah? From which profession?"

Touché. "The legal one."

Bruce guffawed. "The *really* shady one."

He looked ready to make a joke about the connection between prostitutes and lawyers, but I gave him the look that let him know I wasn't in the mood.

He shrugged. "Anyway, so long as you keep to your medications, it doesn't matter how you dress."

"Of course it does." I picked up the pencil and worked on my brows. "It takes a lot of energy to shift. And a lot of concentration to maintain. How I dress can hurt or help the whole operation."

"You want me to wait till you're finished?"

"I'm almost done here," I said. "Go get the black leather briefcase ready."

"Contents?"

"Persona: Jacquelyne Mae. Operation: Interview. Location: Law firm."

Bruce backed out of the doorway and headed toward the den.

I finished my makeup, went into my bedroom, and examined the complete package in the full-length mirror. A custom black dress stopping at the knees, cord belt, and citrine stud earrings. Appropriate for late September. Appropriate for an interview at a law firm. It was a pretty outfit. It would be even prettier when I added the matching jacket and handbag. And my face, when I remade it, would make the entire package absolutely *beautiful.*

But I wasn't quite there yet. Choosing shoes was always difficult. Beauty versus practicality: the former sometimes provided a decisive advantage when confronting certain enemies. Heels would be expected, and they would certainly complement my dress, but at some point I was going to need to break, run, and take some long jumps. Even though I could damn sure move quickly in heels, I couldn't sprint more than fifty meters in them without bruising myself. In some situations, they'd make for nice weapons. For today's job, flats would be more effective once shit hit the fan, but I certainly couldn't wear those to an interview.

Decisions, decisions—pretty, pretty decisions...

I chose black and gold-studded wedge sandals.

"Your briefcase, Miss Mae." Bruce poorly affected the tone of an English butler as he walked into the bedroom and laid the case on the bed next to the handbag. "The papers are inside." He held up his left hand. "Here's the wallet for your purse. Fake license, credit and debit cards, and one hundred and twenty dollars in cash."

"Lay it next to the handbag."

"Will you be needing any accessories?" Bruce asked.

"The thumb drives we discussed last night should be in the briefcase. Just the usual makeup and touch-up perfume in the handbag."

"Already done," Bruce said. "I meant anything sharp and shiny?"

"I'm going in soft," I said. "I *will* have to pass through a metal detector."

"So we're definitely not hitting a pimp this time?"

"A white-collar pimp," I said. "The worst kind."

"Which one from my list?"

"He wasn't on it. His name's Prakul Varman."

Bruce shook his head. "Not a familiar name to me. But you're going into this place to get him... You don't want to wait for him to come outside? Hit him on his way to lunch or coffee?"

"He doesn't get his own coffee. He has one of his girls do it for him—ditzy paralegals and chirping secretaries. Besides, we need to make a *statement*. I need to do it in his office so all his colleagues can see."

"You could just as well do it in his home. Film it, stream it over the internet while you run a blade across his—"

"*Bruce*, this firm is an important link in the chain. I need to get info I can only get from inside. Once we have it—"

"All right, Betty." Bruce nodded. "Got it."

"Besides, seeing the body freshly bled in front of them will be much different than his colleagues seeing it on a screen. Jaded souls, I'm sure they are."

"Yeah." Bruce chuckled. "Jaded souls we *all* are."

"While I'm inside, I'm going to need you to rendezvous with one of the suppliers. Pick up some more of my medications."

"For the skin?" Bruce asked. "Or for what's under?"

"Everything," I said. "I don't ever want to be in short supply of anything. Make your connection then get the car ready. And double check the traffic reports. My interview's at ten. I want to be at least fifteen minutes early."

Bruce left the room.

I opened the briefcase. Thirteen copies of Jacquelyne Mae's resume, five copies of each letter of professional recommendation, three blue pens, two black pens, and one red pen, a notepad, and two thumb drives. Plenty of room to spare for a blade or two, even the kind that wouldn't be picked up by metal detectors or a visual search—but no. Today I was resolved to rely solely on my prettier talents.

I'D SPENT much of the night studying the floor plans and the layout of the neighborhood. I'd obtained the most recent maps the day before. The firm had undergone some internal construction but the layout was pretty much the same as the last time I was there. I went over everything one last time in the car, ensuring I had all possible escape routes memorized.

Bruce said nothing during the drive. He knew I needed to think. I broke the silence when we were about two blocks away from the target.

"Make a right here."

He did as instructed.

"Turn left up ahead then let the car idle," I said, "and keep an eye out."

It was time to complete the look.

I pulled down the visor and looked in the vanity mirror. As I silently recited a chant, my eyes drew in light, sipped it like liquid through a straw, stripped it down to filaments of radiation, and then spun the filaments out like living, coiling, intangible threads under my sole control. The ability to manipulate light was a Virus-carrier's curse or blessing, depending on how the carrier chose to live her life. I put the multitude of "living" light-threads to work on my face— tightening a spot here, re-coloring a spot there, erasing a scar, adding a well-placed freckle or two, making this area more prominent, making that area less so—until I really looked like a *Jacquelyne Mae*. A *beautiful* woman.

My viral condition and the skill I'd acquired to cope with

it enabled me to change the appearance of my face and body with relative ease, and the special makeup allowed me to hold the look for a longer amount of time with a minimal amount of concentration. The susceptible would believe I was the person I wanted them to think I was. The fools in the lawless firm would not only believe the illusion but *love* it.

Bruce whistled as his eyes took in the new me, then he shook his head. "Still seems like a lot of unnecessary trouble, Betty. You could easily turn yourself invisible, sneak in, do the deed, and walk out as, uh, pretty as you please."

I sighed as I pushed up the visor. Poor Bruce was still relatively new to this life. I'd tried my best when training him to be my faithful assistant. He occasionally did offer helpful advice, but oftentimes he just didn't get it. Such was a perk of not being a Virus-carrier.

"Invisibility," I said. "Camouflage. These take greater amounts of concentration and will. They're energy drainers. Once in, I'm going to need to focus on studying the layout. These floor plans were helpful, but this is still slightly unfamiliar territory. And even though I worked here in the past, I can't totally rely on what I once thought to be true."

"The supplier I'm meeting with is Montross," Bruce said. "You know his background. Should I let him in on what's up? His boys could provide backup."

I closed my eyes and sighed again. He still didn't have complete confidence in me. It was kind of sweet in a way, him wanting to ensure I remained safe, especially considering how we first met.

"I know what I'm doing, Bruce. I was trained by... Well, I was trained by some who have more abilities and skills than they have any honest right to have. I'll be better off without meddling."

He nodded. I got out of the car and circled around to his window.

"One day you may get to see me in action," I said, "from start to finish. Then you'll understand how getting in is the hard part. Easing out is relatively sublime."

AS EXPECTED, lobby security was a breeze. Upon reaching fifty-plus employees, most firms and companies in Richmond went through the trouble of hiring security guards and installing metal detectors. Once a business reached fifty employees, ugly elements started to pay attention; if it wasn't ripe for robbing, it might be ripe for exploding. The terrorists, gangs, and cults proliferating the area were always in contention for the biggest score in dollars or body count.

Miss Pruden from Human Resources met me in the lobby's elevator bank. "Miss Jacquelyne Mae?" We shook hands. "So pleased to meet you." She pushed the "up" button. "How has your day been so far?"

"Progressing beautifully," I said.

We stepped inside the elevator. I scanned all four walls then cast my eyes upward. One obvious camera in the back right corner. I shifted my vision across the electromagnetic spectrum as I scanned the roof. Opening the service hatch would be a piece of cake, but I put it on the list of last resorts. I wasn't about to go scrambling around in an elevator shaft again. Not if I could help it.

"I hope you don't mind me saying how impressive your resume is, Miss Mae."

"Why would I mind?" I asked.

She shrugged. "Well, you're no stranger to law firms. You

know that a copy of an interviewee's resume has been given to everyone she's likely to come into contact with."

I nodded. "True."

"But no one's supposed to comment on it except the people with whom you've scheduled interviews."

I smiled and nodded again. "I know how the process works."

"But I just wanted to say how grateful I am for the *pro bono* work you've done on behalf of abused and, uh, *sick* women. Those living in the House of Thomas shelters. People like you are an inspiration."

I lost my smile and swallowed. Residents of the HOT shelters were those with incurable diseases. Generally, only Virus-carriers, those afflicted with other extreme ailments, and liberal do-gooders were sympathetic to the work the shelters performed. My research hadn't led me to conclude anyone employed by this firm would do anyone any good; the item was only on the resume as some volunteer work Jacquelyne Mae had done fresh out of law school, a time when people were expected to do stuff just because it looked good on a resume, not because they actually believed in what they were doing. Was Pruden a Virus-carrier, one adept at hiding her condition, or a bleeding heart who'd slipped through the cracks? If she or anyone else here were a Virus-carrier, a trained one, I'd have to alter my strategy. I looked at her face, looked beneath the skin— x-rayed, magnified, and tried a few other optical tricks as well as I could without seeming blatantly odd. I didn't detect any parasites. She wasn't a carrier, just a bleeding heart. If she crossed my path on my way out, I'd try not to hurt her too badly.

"I try to do my best," I said.

We stopped on the tenth floor.

"You'll be meeting with Miss Shaw first," Pruden said as she led the way past the reception and through the hall. "Then one of the senior associates."

"Any partners?" I asked.

"Well, it's a little unusual for a first round. But, since you have such awesome credentials, maybe Miss Shaw can set something up, depending on schedules. Is there anyone in particular you'd like to try to see?"

"I have one or two in mind." I wasn't about to give anything away and risk losing the element of surprise. "I'll discuss with Miss Shaw."

Surreal artwork covered the walls, all by artists who'd tried hard to one-up or two-up Van Gogh. *Spectacular.* They were vibrant enough for me to use to my advantage if I needed any extra help escaping.

None of the offices I passed had doors, and half were empty. No surprise. The recession had been tough on almost everyone, including this once-mighty firm that in my day had filled all thirteen of its floors. But they weren't hurting that badly. Varman and his department were full of black-rainmakers. They were still bringing in the dollars just fine.

Shaw was a frumpy but seemingly affable woman in her mid to late 40s. I was expecting someone taller, leggier, more *angular*, and wearing just the right skirt and blouse to show off all the goods. Firms of this type usually put women of that sort in the HR and recruitment departments, putting up a good front to attract the right sort of hires. In fact, I would have been willing to bet women of that kind *were* to be found aplenty among this firm's recruiters, but they probably only met with the male prospects.

We exchanged introductions and shook hands. When invited, I sat in the chair in front of her desk and handed her a copy of my resume. Of course, she'd already read it, but she scanned it again, either to refresh her memory or to be polite. Before she could ask her first question, I reached back into my case and said, "Each of my references typed out a brief letter of recommendation. The letters include contact information for follow-up discussions." I handed her one copy of all five, all originally signed, though not by the people whose names were at the top. Bruce wasn't quite a master forger, but he was good enough.

"Impressive," Shaw said. "Most people just provide names, titles, and phone numbers for their references."

"I wanted to go the extra mile."

Shaw skimmed the letters and I skimmed my surroundings.

"So," she said, "you want to be an associate with our firm." She looked me up and down, taking in the entire package before her. "You know the recession has been hard on everyone, especially lawyers..."

Yeah—bullshit time. She asked her questions and I gave her the answers she wanted to hear, justifying my existence and intentions, highlighting my goals and assets, even elaborating with stories and anecdotes so she didn't think I was some robotic candidate reading from a script. I was the perfect interviewee—even though I kind of *was* reading from a script, paying less attention to our conversation than to my more immediate task of drilling into her mind. My gaze never left her eyes as we talked. I'd established contact when answering her first question by subtly lighting the tissue of my irises like a firefly's abdomen. That very sight coupled with the sound of my voice was the hook, and with each subsequent question and answer, a fraction of my consciousness drilled deeper and deeper past her eyes and into her mind. I needed to go deep enough so that, when I planted a certain suggestion, I'd set off a psychosomatic reaction, making a mere wish come true.

Fifteen minutes into the interview, I was deep enough. Her breakfast, only partially digested, wasn't sitting well—so I thought... so *she* thought... The mush wanted out of her. Something in her bowels shifted, making a rumble loud enough for us both to hear. I didn't react when she grimaced; I just kept on answering her question about Jacquelyne Mae's charity work.

There was another rumble and another grimace before she said, "Uh, Miss Mae, pardon me for interrupting, but if you'll excuse me for one second, there's something I must check on."

She stood and walked quickly toward the door, her arms pressed to her sides.

I didn't have a lot of time. Luckily, I didn't require much.

I remained in my chair as I shifted the light around me, creating a thick shell of myself—the appearance of myself—sitting in the chair, stiffly, waiting patiently for Shaw to return. Then I stepped out of the illusion, bending the light surrounding my real body, making it invisible to the camera I'd seen in the ceiling and any others I might have missed.

Some people can easily divide their attention. They can listen to a speech while reading a book on a wildly different subject and retain everything they've seen and heard. I had been trained to do something similar when it came to manipulating electromagnetic radiation. But, as all tricks required physical and mental energy, they were necessarily time-limited. My out-of-body trick would expire in roughly ten minutes.

I took the two drives out of my bag and made for Shaw's computer. I inserted the first one into a USB port. Acquired from one of Bruce's contacts, the drive was first-class spy technology. It worked at lightning speed to download specific information from a computer and any other computers connected to it. Firewalls and all other security measures—at least those used by most in the public sector —were of no consequence. All one had to do was plug it in, sit back, and let it extract. In sixty seconds it was halfway done.

But someone was approaching Shaw's office.

Pruden. *Shit.*

I couldn't stop now, and I couldn't retake my position in the chair.

Pruden entered the office. "Miss Mae? Can I get you anything while you're waiting for Miss Shaw? Coffee? Water?"

Throwing my voice was one trick I'd never learned, surprisingly. I was one of the few ex-Sprytes who wasn't a singer, not even a bad one, and I'd left the fold before I could ever learn. So I'd have to do this the dirty way.

Maintaining invisibility, I got behind Pruden as she cautiously approached the hologram, no doubt wondering why it wasn't moving or responding to her. I put my right hand firmly over her mouth and placed my left arm across her neck tightly enough so she'd be unable to move as I leaned in and whispered a rhyming, alliterative chant. After ten seconds, I released her, letting her collapse on the floor, unconscious and invisible. Singing lessons, no—but I had taken the witch's poetry lessons and mastered them.

I dragged the invisible woman into a corner so she'd be out of the way when I broke and ran, then I rushed to the computer, unplugged the first drive, and inserted the second. More top-notch technology, this one would install malware into the firm's system. When I was long gone it would also leave a message, letting everyone know why

Varman had been targeted and warning all others of the same filthy ilk.

Someone else was approaching the door.

Shaw.

And the second drive didn't seem to be working.

Fuck it.

I left the drive where it was and hustled to grab my briefcase and handbag.

Shaw entered the office. "I apologize Miss Mae, but I—" She turned and saw Pruden's slumped body in the corner. "What—?"

I'd released the concentration needed to keep Pruden unseen. I needed it for my next trick.

I got in front of Shaw and dropped my own veil of invisibility. She whipped her gaze from Pruden to me. I could see it in her eyes—she was ready to release a scream that would be heard halfway down the hall. I grabbed the back of her neck with my left hand as I jammed the heel of my right under her jaw. Shaw instinctively shut her eyes, tight.

"Listen carefully," I said before launching into another chant. This one wouldn't render the woman unconscious or invisible. Quite the opposite. It would leave her calm, awake, and alert enough to respond to any questions with some variant of "Nothing is wrong. Please leave me alone."

I felt her body relax. It was working. When her eyes opened, I knew it had worked. I led her to her chair, sat her down comfortably, then retrieved my briefcase and handbag.

The hologram of myself was fading. Shaw's trance would last for just thirty minutes, and the trick would only work if potential visitors didn't progress far enough past her doorway to notice Pruden.

My first instinct was to make myself invisible again, but I

needed to conserve energy. I'd spent enough already without even seeing my target. Plus, with my hologram now dissipated, onlookers might wonder where I'd disappeared to.

I nonchalantly walked out of Shaw's office, visible and ready to flash a broad smile at anyone who made eye contact. I'd gone maybe a dozen steps before I had a thought: the ceiling camera in Shaw's office. Surely security had seen me assault Shaw, even if they'd missed me taking out Pruden. *Green mistake.* I quickened my pace.

I always opted for stairs when I could. Elevators were never safe havens, not even temporary ones. Besides, it was easier to fight and deceive one's way through a stairwell. Easier for me, anyway. I located the nearest exit sign and followed it.

I pushed through the door then paused, listening for voices. The stairwell was empty—for the moment. The security guards' office was on the seventh floor. My target was on the thirteenth. I ran up the stairs, appreciating the symbolism as I moved. "Mae" began with the thirteenth letter, and "Jacquelyne Mae" had thirteen letters. All would work to my advantage. The witch had been clever in seasoning her acolytes with all sorts of magicks that relied heavily on the placement of numbers and letters. When I stepped out of the stairwell, I felt I was in the zone. The floor seemed to bounce a little under my feet, as if I were lightly jogging on a resilient running track. And that's how I moved, hustling like an employee running late for a meeting.

There were just as many empty offices on this floor as there had been on ten. The people I did see hardly gave me a second look as I moved. Well, many of the men did, but not because they were suspicious.

My target was in office 13-8, a corner office. As I approached, I heard Varman's voice and that of another man's. Both were equally angry about something.

There was more than one person, and they were both agitated. That wouldn't be a problem. I could probably blind and choke Varman's guest out before—

"Can I help you?"

I paused, shuddering a little before turning in the direction of the woman's voice. I expected a secretary, but the woman wasn't sitting at one of the nearby stations. She was standing just a few feet behind me and wearing a security guard's uniform. Blonde, close-cropped hair; mid 40s; maybe ex-cop or ex-military; not in the best shape, but could probably handle herself well enough. I'd been so focused on Varman's doorway I didn't even realize someone was focusing on me. *Second green mistake.* I couldn't afford a third.

"I, uhm... I have an appointment to meet with Mister Varman."

"How's that? Do you work here?"

"I—" She was going to ask for my firm identification card next, so best not to lie. "No. I used to a long time ago, but I'm interviewing today and I wanted to—"

"*Interviewing*? You don't work here? How are you walking the halls without an escort?" With each question, her voice got louder, drawing more attention. She raised her walkie-talkie, which made onlookers pay even sharper attention.

There was nothing I could say or do to stun her, not with so many eyes on us. Turning invisible was out of the question. So I gambled on option number three.

"Listen," I said, "please don't say anything. I'm his niece, and I was going to surprise him."

The security guard paused.

"We haven't seen each other or even spoken in years," I said, "not since my family lost everything in the typhoon and he sent us some money to get by. Now that I've finished law school, near the top of my class... Well, I didn't want to gamble on whether or not I'd get a job here. I may or may not. I just want to surprise him, let him know how instrumental his money was in getting me to where I am today."

The guard was old enough to be a mother. Whether she was or she wasn't, she undoubtedly had some sympathy for family matters. Cops and military types, the female ones, were like that. And even though I wasn't a musician, I sure knew how to play heartstrings.

"Okay," she said. "Go ahead, but you really should be escorted. I'll wait out here to walk you back when you're finished."

I clasped my hands in front of my face and nodded. "Thank you." I turned and continued my approach, aware that the security guard's eyes were trained on me the whole time. There was still a chance she was going to call someone on that walkie-talkie. I had to be quick.

Varman and whoever else was in his office were still engaged in a heated discussion. I wasn't sure what they were talking about, and I didn't much care at this point.

I stepped into the doorway. Varman saw me and stopped mid-argument.

"Who the fu—?"

His guest, seated in front of his desk, turned and glared. An older man in a suit, in his 50s, undoubtedly another partner.

"I apologize for interrupting," I said, "but I just had to see you before I left the building—*Uncle*."

Varman straightened a little. He'd gotten the reference.

"Uncle" meant one thing to the likes of the security guard and something entirely different to the likes of Varman. It was a code word—a damned, dirty, *disgusting* word that sounded pleasant to the disgusting likes of him.

"May I come in?" I asked.

Varman nodded slowly. He got a better look at me under his office lights. His brow unfurrowed and his grimace twisted like a worm to take the shape of a smile. "Hello..." If worms could talk, they'd sound like this slimeball. He didn't even have enough charm to evoke a snake. It was just as well. It's so *easy* to kill slimy things.

"Prakul," the man in the chair said, "who is this woman? We're not finished discussing the—"

"This is family, I believe," Varman said. "I'm sure you agree family takes precedence over... over what we were discussing. I'll give you a call, Mark. Please close the door behind you."

Mark stood and tossed me a nasty glance as he passed. Age notwithstanding, Varman was clearly the senior partner.

"What can I do for you, *niecey*?"

"I'll tell you what I've told the others before I settled their accounts." I approached deliberately as my eyes drew in light, dimming his office with each step. "There is a ring of pimps in the greater Richmond area, malicious abductors who've taken women—*girls*—and drugged them, kept them high, kept them captive against their will. When arrested, none of these rodents can manage to stay in jail, despite mountains of evidence. They seem to have lawyers on top of lawyers."

Varman was too entranced, too frightened, or too confused to move.

"My research tells me you're one of the ones on top," I

said. "A sugar uncle. An *Uncle Sugar*. I got it. I got that twisted joke long ago... A twisted *U.S.A.* A shadowy government fueled by drugs and prostitution. You're a big part of the judicial branch, the supreme court of this shadowy bullshit. But on the surface, in the *light*, you're just a lawyer keeping big-time pimps and pushers out of jail. Apparently, you've been performing all your work for them *pro bono*. I'm not going to bother asking the why of it all. I don't have time to listen to your greasy lies. A slick computer program will tell me all I need to know about *all* the slicksters."

Varman's smile was a distant memory. I saw it in his eyes —he wasn't sure whether to reach for his phone or yell for help. I made sure he did neither by keeping my glowing eyes locked on his as I dropped my handbag and briefcase.

"Who are you?" He spoke in a near-whisper. "*Really* who are you?"

"I'm the one who's going to snuff out your shadow. I'm the one who's going to use you as an example that I can get to *anyone* in your fraudulent government at any time. The injustice system in this area may not care about your kind, for whatever reason, but I do—and I'm going to make your putrid kind extinct."

Varman's hand flinched as he drew in a breath, his mouth opening wider. He was going to scream and reach for his phone. I flared my eyes, unleashing every bit of light stolen from the pitch-black office, shoving everything from my eyes into his. He screamed all right.

That security guard would barge in at any moment. I ran, jumped onto the desk, grabbed a stapler and swiveled just as she entered. I tossed the stapler to my left, enveloping it in crafted light, making it appear as a parrot. Confused, the guard turned her head, keeping her eyes on the distraction as I tossed a cluster of infrared pellets toward the side of her face. She screamed as she fell, hitting her head in just the right way against the doorframe, knocking herself unconscious.

That last bit was luck. I was afraid I'd have to spend a few precious seconds throttling her while whispering poetry into her ear.

I turned back toward Varman. He was writhing on the floor behind his desk, grasping at anything within reach. I'd attempted to fry his optic nerves, probably blinding him for life—not that he had much of it left to live anyway.

I hopped down, turned him on his back, and sat on his sternum, pinning his arms under my knees. I grasped the top of his head with my fingers and placed my thumbs over his eyelids. He kept screaming, but I made sure he heard me.

"I've been saving a special poem for you, vermin."

I applied pressure with my thumbs as I recited it. In the back of my mind, I knew security was rushing toward the office. Someone may've even called the police. A wannabe hero among the office staff had probably gathered up some courage and a broomstick and was heading this way. Didn't matter at this point. My poem was a short one, carefully composed with elements of Varman's name, behaviors, and biography. By the time I reached the sixth line, the struggle had left him. When I reached the eighth, his bones were hollow. At the eleventh, his skin was thin as rice paper. At the twelfth and final line, I twisted my wrists, inserting my thumbs completely, and heard the *hiss*.

I stood up. There were voices behind me, near the doorway. The most prominent one yelled, "Don't move!" I didn't. I didn't even turn to see who'd said it.

But Varman moved. And I'm sure whoever was behind me watched his body float upward and turn face down, its arms and legs splayed, its irradiated skin emitting a glow that inspired hopelessness while the mouth gaped, vomiting a putrid stream of blood, liquefied organs, and stuff even a seasoned crime scene specialist would be too repulsed to try to identify.

Once the body stuck to the ceiling, unable to ascend any further, I turned to see if anyone was still there, still staring. Only two men in suits, possibly senior associates. Both were watching Varman's body, not mine. I could get by them easily, but—hell—why not go out with a little style?

I hopped onto the desk, grabbed a tape dispenser and a ceramic cup full of pens, and tossed them. Flying creatures of light and the mummifying corpse on the ceiling had the two lawyers looking everywhere but at me. I punched and kicked them as I passed, hitting them both in spots sweet enough to ensure they wouldn't get up and follow me anytime soon.

I retrieved my handbag and briefcase and stepped outside the office. Two empty secretarial stations were in front of me. There was a hallway to my left and a hallway to my right. Security guards were coming fast down both of them. They didn't have guns or Tasers, but like the sleeping blonde in the office behind me, they appeared to be either ex-cop or ex-military. Trained.

But trained by mere men, not by a witch.

I tossed my bag and briefcase onto one of the secretary's desks then loosened the cord belt around my waist. My dress went loose as my skin sapped all available light in the vicinity.

I didn't gradually dim the lights this time. I *zapped* them off and made myself appear as an aglow *angel* in the eyes of these men who surely entertained ideas both sexist and sexual.

As expected, they didn't retreat. They pressed on toward me, intending to tackle and do who-the-hell knew what else. *Good*—just as long as they kept their eyes *on* me, particularly on my *pretty* face, which was now the most prominent part of me.

When they were all within ten feet, I pulled back my hair and directed all the light my skin had gathered toward my ears and into my citrine earrings, where the light strengthened before splaying outward.

To say I simply dazzled them wouldn't do me justice— but I meted sufficient justice to the guards. They weren't permanently harmed. They'd wake up in an hour or two. And the outer layers of skin on their faces would probably heal in a couple of weeks.

I retrieved my bags yet again and cut left, toward the stairwell I'd used earlier. Three or four brave-but-foolish souls stepped out of their offices, either to try to understand the source of commotion or to put a stop to it. I put a stop to whatever notions anyone had when I snapped my belt across their faces.

It hadn't been necessary to make the paintings come alive after all.

I barreled through the stairwell door and scrambled up the steps. Not wearing heels had been a wise move. I ascended with relative ease.

The police had undoubtedly arrived by now. They and the rest of the security guards would be in the lobby and on the streets surrounding the building. No one would guess the perpetrator of all this chaos would head to the roof. Who in their right mind would do so?

I didn't stop running until I actually tasted fresh air. I tightened the straps of my briefcase and my handbag, then used my belt to secure them even tighter to my abdomen.

My research had told me the east side of the building would provide an easier jump. I checked my bags again to ensure they were securely fastened, then I hustled.

I rounded the elevator bank and stopped—*cold*.

It felt as though I'd walked into a freezer naked. I shivered but couldn't take another step as I gazed ahead at Miss Pruden, gazing back at me.

"The police are the least of your worries," she said.

"Who's worried?" I asked. Pruden was unexpected, but she didn't scare me—though my chattering teeth no doubt gave her the contrary impression. "I just took out a menace to society." I tilted my trembling head backward and cast my eyes in the direction of the sun. I stopped shivering. "Guess I'm about to take out another one." I lowered my head and met her eyes.

Pruden approached. "You've interfered with a federal investigation, bitch."

I had goose bumps. My extremities were tingling. I may've been able to move my arms or legs, but I didn't.

"I knew you weren't here to get hired," Pruden continued, "but I knew you were here for some kind of *job*. I tried to research you, tried to figure out who you're with. I initially assumed the IAI—but, no. You're too sophisticated. My best guess? You're one of those Arkangel bitches."

The tingling had subsided but I still didn't move, even as Pruden got within ten feet of me.

"I know you won't tell me," I said, "so I won't bother asking—but whoever you're with, they were moving too slowly. As far as I'm concerned, you're aiding and abetting the enemy."

"Dumb bitch. You have no idea how federal investigations work."

"I know how *my* investigations work," I said. "And I

know what it means for one woman to repeatedly call another a 'bitch.' "

We were now no more than five feet from one another, staring eye to eye. There were many different types of Virus-carriers, and among those were many different threat-levels. What kind of medication or drugs did Pruden take? What type of training had she undergone? Did she have a mentor? If so, how vicious and sadistic was she?

I hadn't done the research on her that she'd try to do on me, and I couldn't even guess what cult or clique she'd come from—that ice-light method she used was new to me—but I did know one thing. She was brazen or stupid enough to get this close, look me in the eye, and leave her ears uncovered.

"You have a problem with the word, *bitch*?" Pruden said. "Tough. I call 'em like I see 'em."

"So do I." I dilated my pupils and released a piercing wail to accompany the spillage of light I'd gathered from the sun.

The woman tumbled backward as if hit by a water cannon. I didn't wait to see her try to get to her feet. I ran, gathering speed as I neared the edge of the roof, then leapt off.

While airborne, my specially designed dress and matching jacket reconfigured slightly and combined with my electromagnetic talents to provide enough lift for me to glide to the next building, eleven stories tall. I sprinted across the roof and jumped off the next edge, using the same talents to glide across to the roof of a building roughly the same size. I ran and jumped off the ledge once more, this time letting myself miss the roof and fall a couple stories down, landing relatively unscathed on the fire escape.

Now safely out of sight of the city's flying drones and all the surrounding buildings' cameras, I hustled down the stairs as I monitored my surroundings and modified the appearance of my face, skin tone, and clothes. I retrieved the malodorous perfume from my purse and sprayed it strategically. I then retrieved a bottle of brown and black powder and applied it deftly to my clothes. By the time I hit the ground, Jacquelyne Mae had been put to rest. Walking in her place was a reeking, dirty, wrinkly old bag lady who shuffled along from trashcan to trashcan.

I knew all the drones, cameras, and humans around me would be all too willing to turn a blind eye to what I'd become.

I SMOOTHED the harsh edges and freshened up before meeting Bruce twenty blocks away from the target area. Our rendezvous was a small tea house that sat quietly away from all high-traffic roads. Bruce had undoubtedly cased the place already, but I did the same before going inside.

He was sitting at a two-person table in the back left corner. He'd ordered us the dragon green tea. I could tell by my cup's lack of steam that Bruce had poured it more than ten minutes before I'd arrived. He had either arrived really early or was just unusually impatient today.

I handed him the one thumb drive I had left. He slipped it inside his jacket pocket without looking at it, keeping his eyes on mine as he asked, "Status of target?"

"Terminated." I picked up my cup and sipped. *Yeah* —lukewarm.

He picked up his cup. "Complications?"

"Encountered one carrier. Unknown classification. Possibly HSA, undercover agent."

Bruce furrowed his brow but said nothing. He simply

sipped and cast his eyes around the room. Funny. He wasn't hard to read. Hearing mention of the Heartland Security Agency, he probably figured we might be stepping out of our league. Him looking around was a signal that we were possibly someplace we shouldn't be—but in a literal sense it wasn't true. The tea house was empty at this hour. And the owner and his employees were all old friends of his, highly trusted by him when he had been a detective.

"We're fine," I said. "Nothing to worry about."

Bruce looked at me. "The thumb drive?"

"Should contain every email sent and received by everyone at the firm over the last ninety days. When we get back you'll need to search for keywords and then cross-reference any names on your old list."

Bruce nodded. "The other one?"

"Not sure it worked. But I left it in, just in case. I got surprised and had to get out."

"And leave them your thumb print," Bruce said. "I told you you should start wearing gloves."

I chuckled. "Yeah. Wearing gloves to an interview makes sense."

"They can run your prints. The right person... the *wrong* people will be able to trace—"

"My original identity is dead, Bruce. Let them try."

"Your new HSA friend will try, you better believe it." He sipped and cast his eyes around again, this time with good reason. Two patrons had walked in. A male and a female, early college age, both wearing dull expressions. I doubted they were any kind of threat, but maybe Bruce had other ideas. He wouldn't take his eyes off them.

"Let's head back," I said. "I want you to get started on that information. And I need to plan for tomorrow."

We left cash on the table and walked toward the front

exit. Both of us glanced at the college kids on the way out. The female glanced back, but the male paid us no attention whatsoever. They wouldn't be a problem.

Outside, Bruce looked around and said in a lowered voice, "The medications are in the car. You want to take it?"

"Where are you going?"

"Might be a good idea for us to split up"—he again looked over his shoulders—"I know you've been careful and all. But I don't like this HSA business."

I didn't like the fact I hadn't been able to detect Pruden as a carrier when we shared the elevator. She was a variant —that much was clear. But what would the HSA want with her? Why would they plant *her* there instead of a clean agent? Hell, it was probably for the same reason I waltzed in there so easily. The woman was more handsome than undeniably beautiful, but there was no denying she was attractive in all the right ways. Whether that was a trick of light and makeup or just actual fact didn't matter. People would listen when she wanted to tell them something; people would open doors for her, pull out chairs for her... let her open files, let her easily pull out secrets.

"The HSA is probably investigating this so-called shadow government, too," I said. "So what? That's what they're supposed to be doing. But their intentions don't matter. They're so tangled up in their own red tape, they're tripping over it. That's the inevitable nature of bureaucracy. That's why I work solo."

Bruce cocked his head.

"You know what I mean," I said.

The two college kids came out of the tea house. We both watched as they walked. The girl again glanced in our direction—twice—while the boy seemed to pay no mind. I felt less easy about them now, less easy about *her*. If I'd learned anything over the past few years, it was that teenage girls on the cusp of adulthood could be big trouble. But the two simply got into their car and drove away. It was time we did the same.

"We're *not* splitting up," I said.

Bruce shrugged. "Okay, Betty. Have it your way."

I followed him to the alley where he had parked the town car, out of the sight of drones and cameras. I looked around while Bruce ensured the car hadn't been tampered with. We then got in and drove off, keeping off the main roads as much as possible.

"You'd be wise to be wary of the HSA," Bruce said after we'd gone a couple of blocks. "You know my old department worked with them on a couple of cases? Some of those guys, they're not all that they seem."

"Whatever they are," I said. "I've seen worse." *Much* worse—even before I contracted the sexually transmitted Virus.

A burning for social justice had flared up in me at a young age after seeing the way my father treated my step-mother, someone to whom I logically should have felt little connection and even less loyalty. But maybe those early flames were too bright. I made it through college without a clear idea of what I wanted to do with myself. I'd spent my energy studying and arguing and only found relief from the constant stress by learning yoga and massage therapy. Straight-up meditation was a no-go for me. At the end of four years, I'd gained knowledge and weight, but I'd no better sense of place, no wisdom. I only felt bloated: fat and overstuffed on liberal arts.

Going to law school was the fashionable path for wayward college grads, a route to job security if not happi-ness. My first semester there was rough, but during the second I met a teenage girl, a very charming girl who despite her young age was acquainted with some of my female classmates. She provided them, and eventually me, with supplements that increased awareness and made it easier to focus. Those damned, sweet pills made me sensitive in so many ways...

That's how I ended up sleeping with the wrong guy.

In my third year, when I first exhibited violent symptoms of the White Fire Virus, I again met the girl. She was strolling the hospital halls. At first, I thought it was just chance, but later—much too late—I figured it was by design. She told me she had other supplements—some deep, *deep* black market stuff—that could help me cope with my new condition and eventually master it. Not only would my life not be ruined, but it could change for the better. I could finish law school, feeling as healthy as before, and as laser-focused as before. But there was one catch. The girl wanted me to engage in extracurricular studies with her and her circle of friends twice a week, and then four times a week after I graduated.

The way the supplements made me feel, I was happy to agree to anything. I was just as happy to land a job practicing corporate law after graduating in the upper tier of my class. But, out of all lawyers, the recession was most ruthless to the corporate ones. I held the job for the same amount of time most people stay on their honeymoon. At the charming girl's behest, I began spending more time with her and her associates—the Ladies of the Light, as she sometimes referred to us en masse, and quite ironically, as much of that time it seemed as if my head was in a fog. I don't clearly remember the initiation process. Hell, I don't even remember fully agreeing to become part of some magickal cult. Nonetheless, I ended up as a Spryte, a living weapon and instrument for the witch Carmilla, the so-called Girl of Many Charms.

Unlike the other women who'd totally fallen under her spell, though, I was never fully in line. And after one particularly ugly incident, I broke free. The witch had trained me well enough so that I could cover my tracks and stay hidden. But I couldn't confine myself to a cave for the rest of my life. I needed a decent place to stay. I'd have to pay rent, and I'd have to eat. I couldn't apply for a job in my profession, not even as a paralegal or a document reviewer. That would've made it too easy for Carmilla to find me. So I resorted to using the talents I'd long ago acquired in order to put myself through college: giving therapeutic massages to anyone willing to pay. I was certified as a massage therapist, but few seemed to care so long as I untangled the knots in their muscles and rubbed their stress away.

And yet the amount I earned as a run-of-the-mill CMT just wasn't cutting it. There's no shortage of stressed out folks during a recession, but many were extremely careful about how they spent their money. Still, I had customers, and I liked what I did. I liked it even more when I discovered finishing off with a happy ending led to much bigger tips. Twisting my technique so that the massage was sensuous from beginning to end allowed me to double my price and increase my clientele.

It was all highly illegal but, as Bruce constantly joked, it was also more honest than what most lawyers did. I'd met him during this time in my life. He was the lead detective in charge of breaking up a sex trafficking ring in the Richmond area. For some reason or another, one of the pimps he'd rounded up had my number stored in their smartphone. Maybe I had unwittingly given one of them a massage, or maybe one of them had found my number on a "good rubs" site and had saved it with the intention of recruiting me. Whatever—Bruce tracked me down by himself. He confronted me and interrogated me on the spot, gazing into my sepia eyes...

He slid into the palms of my hands—*beautifully*. I helped the detective see the reasons behind my way of life. Soon after, he turned in his badge, telling his superiors he was going to work in the private sector. With a wry smile he told them he was going to be a private dick. Together we found a safe place off the radar of both our former overseers, then I helped him continue his investigation. It soon became *my* investigation as I dug deeper and deeper into the dirt, and the detective who'd been repurposed into my valet helped me take out the garbage.

Now the HSA might have gotten involved. The Heartland Security Agency's mission was to protect America's children and preserve traditional families. More than any other government agency, they were tasked with strengthening the country's moral fiber, a key factor in keeping America stronger than any other country. They should've known about this ring and broken it up long before I ever even heard of it.

We stayed silent during the drive, but the expression on Bruce's face and his occasional sighs made it clear he was preoccupied with the thought that the HSA was aware of our vigilante escapades and might confront us. The man was an open book.

We took a shortcut through yet another long alley as I said, "Nothing to worry about—"

"The *fuck*?" Bruce slammed on the brakes as he shouted.

A Lamborghini had sped out in front of us and blocked our way.

It was time to worry.

"Back—" I began, but the former detective didn't need any prompt from me. He'd already put it in reverse and floored it. He stopped at another intersection, no doubt wondering whether to turn right or left. He had only a split second to ponder as we saw a Ferrari speeding from the left, a Jaguar from the right, and a Porsche coming up fast from the rear.

"Shit!" He switched gears and pushed the accelerator, speeding forward. But the Lamborghini had turned into the alley and was heading straight for us. An Aston Martin was right behind it.

Bruce slowed the car; he was beginning to panic. An open book... He was contemplating a game of chicken.

"Stop the car," I said.

"What? I—"

"*Stop* the car," I repeated. "Put it in park."

He did. The other cars stopped as well.

I'd immediately recognized the vehicles' style. All were sleek, brightly colored, armor-plated, and engineered to go much faster than the models available on the public market. I had a sudden and brief regret for the loss of my Corvette Stingray. But even that wouldn't have gotten me out of this.

I opened my door. "Stay in the car—"

"Are you crazy!" Bruce interrupted. "What're you—"

"*Stay* in the car," I repeated. "They're five of them. One in each vehicle. They're too narrow to bother with passengers, and they'll leave you alone if you don't try to antagonize them. So just stay in; I'll draw them away. When I've got them occupied, you get out and run."

"I—"

"Don't question it. Not now." I got out of the car. "Make your way back home—*smartly*. I'll explain everything then, if you want to hear it... and if I make it back."

"What? You—"

I slammed the door, ignoring whatever Bruce was yelling about. I walked toward the rear of the town car and kept on going, casual but careful about my surroundings, ready to defend myself. Trying to break for it would've been stupid. The ladies could run as fast as tigers if need be.

The driver's side doors of the luxury cars all opened at once. The ladies stepped out and moved forward like fashion models on a video shoot. Their appearance matched their movements. All were well over six feet tall. I was so focused on their slinking bodies, I didn't notice whether they'd even closed the car doors behind them.

As they approached, I turned in a circle, watching them, sizing them up, until they stopped, placing me at the center of their circle. The five of them stood equidistant from each other and from me... like five points in a pentagram.

Shit.

I didn't recognize them, but it was clear the witch had trained these Sprytes well.

"Barbara," the bob-cut brunette said, "I believe this is she. Confirm?"

"I confirm," replied the one with the wavy red hair. "What are your eyes telling you, Brittany?"

"My nose is telling me more," said the one with the hime cut. "What do you think, Beverly?"

"No question the skunk is intimate with this one," the pixie-cut blonde answered. "I believe we've found our woman, Bellissa."

"A happy reunion," said the dark chick with the finger wave, "and yet she looks so sad. You'd think she'd be relieved for the opportunity to get clean again, right Bethany?"

"Some of the dirty don't know they're dirty," the brunette said, "until they're clean enough to smell the flowers."

I chuckled away my nervousness as I looked at each of them in turn. "What, no *Brunhilda* among you? Carmilla must be losing her sense of twisted humor."

"You're the one who's lost, Beatrice," Beverly said.

"The Mistress sent us to retrieve you," Bethany said.

"I figured," I said. "I also figured Carmilla knew I wanted nothing more to do with her. Thought I made that clear when I stuck my Stingray into that hideous statue of her." I turned as I spoke, trying to keep my eyes on each of them. "The moniker's 'Betty' now, by the way. I really have declared my independence."

"And yet," Brittany said, "you're using magick that does not belong to you."

"I'm using what I learned while she used me," I said, "while she used *all* of us as bait." I shook my head. "You dumb, beautiful, zombies... The witch tied us up in strings of lies and dipped our souls into another dimension, not giving a damn about us. I got out in time, but you... Your bodies ended up distorted, stretched. You can't think a thought without her approving it first. And all for what? What do you get out of it?"

Their answers ran counterclockwise.

"We were all born again."

"Attaining wisdom."

"Understanding."

"*Power*."

"And the promise of eternal life."

"*Bullshit*," I said. "Carmilla destroys pieces of your soul every time she uses you. You're all too far gone to understand anything. She keeps the real power for *herself*. If her prophecy is even partially true, if there is a life waiting for us—for you—after all this, it will only be as her eternal slaves. I'd rather devote myself to this world, *freeing* slaves. I don't belong to her, and if you weren't under her noxious spell, you'd realize you shouldn't either."

"Beatrice—"

"*Stop* calling me that." They were trying to exercise a form of magick known colloquially as Verbalism. Word Magick. All five of the women had names or, more likely, *pseudonyms* that began with the letter B and had three syllables. One simple purpose in adopting such names was to disorient their targets. Another was to acquire, share, and redouble their power. The action of introducing themselves out loud and accepting their given name in turn sealed a bond, making the ladies more powerful as a whole. And if I, at the center of their circle, accepted a name that fell into that same category as theirs, they'd gain a nearly unbreakable psychological hold over me. I'd used a similar form of magick with Bruce. I changed my original name to click with his, but his name had only one syllable. I had allowed him *some* agency to think and act for himself.

In unison, the five women took two steps closer, tightening the circle. These Sprytes were good, but I'd learned more than a few tricks during my brief tenure as one of them. I spread my fingers and tensed my forearms. They undoubtedly heard the crackle of static as loudly as I. They had the additional treat of seeing the tangles of multihued light pulse under my skin.

"We're not here to fight you, Beatrice," Bethany said.

"Just to warn you," Barbara said.

"And make you an offer," Bellissa said.

Bethany said, "Return to the fold by noon tomorrow, and all will be forgiven."

"Return by dawn," Brittany said, "and all will be forgotten."

"But miss either deadline," Beverly said, "and the Mistress will be forced to send Hunters next time instead of Gatherers."

I glanced over at the town car. The driver's door was open. Bruce was gone.

"And where exactly would I go?" I asked.

"Any of the Mistress's properties," Barbara said. "Once you step foot on one, she'll know you're there."

"But if you're not in place when time is up—"

"Your soul will end up out of time."

"In *no* place."

"What will have been the point of your life then?"

They each backed up four steps before turning their backs to me and slinking back toward their cars. I didn't move until they'd driven away.

The witch had found me, and she could find me again. But I had a choice. Unlike the ladies speeding away, I still had free will, and a conscience.

BY THE TIME I returned home, Bruce was already hard at work. He was so focused on his screen, he only noticed I was a few feet behind him when I coughed.

He stood and turned, reaching for his gun. He was more jittery than usual—but I didn't flinch. When he recognized me, he took a deep breath and put his hands on my shoulders. I kept mine at my side.

"Did they hurt you?" he asked.

"Not physically," I said. "They just gave me a few things

to think about. They... They're—" Something was wrong with my tongue.

Bruce tightened his grip as he looked into my eyes and shook his head. "I know it's not something you're ready to talk about. That's fine. But I have something we should discuss." He let go and nodded toward his laptop. "I haven't gotten through all of it, or even most of it, but look at what I found..." He sat. "Several emails between a high-ranking HSA official and Varman."

I leaned over his shoulder. I no longer felt tongue-tied.

"I'd think an HSA official would be more careful about covering his tracks," I said. "Varman, too, for that matter."

"Maybe someone was just overconfident about the promises of attorney-client privilege."

I snorted. "Yeah. What were they discussing?"

"Politics. Religion. And something about a voluptuous fifteen-year-old redheaded girl that the HSA official wanted to *buy* in order to, and I'm quoting, add to his collection."

"Looks like I have my next target."

Bruce smiled. "Thought you'd say that. So get this..." He punched keys, moving through screens at a rapid pace. "The guy is getting married tomorrow."

"Where?"

"Here." A picture of a beautiful vineyard appeared on his screen. "It's up in Loudoun County."

"Time?"

"Eleven a.m."

Eleven in the morning... *One* and *one* next to each other, in mourning... I immediately began planning my strategy. I had my name and outfit already picked out. I just wondered if I should slit the guy's throat when he started to say "I do," or when his misguided trollop did. Or maybe when they kissed?

"It's at least a two-hour drive," Bruce said. "We'll have to wake up around three or so."

"I'm heading up tonight," I said. "It'll be smarter and more efficient for me to scout the territory well before dawn. In the meantime, I want to know everything I can about this guy. Everything about him, his would-be bride, the guest list, the vineyard, and the surrounding terrain."

"*Really*? All that before you leave?"

"Contact some of your friends. Call in some favors. Do whatever. I'll pack my own clothes and accessories. Have me what you can before I leave and be ready to send me the rest by five a.m."

I hoped I was doing a good job of covering my anxiety. I didn't want to be anywhere near Richmond by dawn. And I didn't want to think about the Sprytes. Only by concentrating fully on my next target could I put them out of my mind.

"Is any of this going to be a problem?" I asked.

He stared at me, the corners of his mouth turning downward.

"Have you ever considered you might be on the wrong track?" he asked. "Or... or just going too fast down the rails? Or—"

"Or maybe *off* the rails?" I said. "Was that what you were about to say?"

He gaped at me for a moment then shook his head. "No. None of this will be a problem."

IT WOULD BE my first time crashing a wedding, but there wasn't too much I needed to plan. It was outdoors. Getting in would be easy. Getting out, almost as easy.

I'd worn a tan brown war-dress, an outfit designed by one of Carmilla's acolytes and inspired by some characters in her favorite book of narrative poetry. The outfit was reinforced in all the right areas to help one fend off bullets, fire, and blades. A woman who really knew how to wear it would look fantastic while dancing, fighting, or simply standing still—but the belt was what really completed the package. It was a fashion accessory that could hold some pretty nice accessories. Mine holstered a pair of nine-inch blades.

The winery had three buildings, all converted barns, and one of them had been prettied up enough to serve as living quarters. Rows and rows of vines surrounded them; heavily forested hills were not much farther out. Making myself invisible would be a snap in the daylight, and switching to camouflage among the trellised vines would be no harder than two snaps. Escaping into the woods would be child's play.

Presently I was camouflaged and positioned comfortably in a tree with a good view. Bruce had sent most of the remaining research I'd requested to my smartphone by dawn. The HSA rat was marrying some tart nearly half his age. Bruce had trouble getting me much info on her background, and he had even more trouble getting details on the guest list. Best he could tell me was that most attendees would be friends of the groom and coworkers of the bride.

I digested pieces of information as I watched the organizers set up. I could've moved in closer but I preferred to stay put, doing my best to keep the branches and leaves around me still while using any and all optical tricks to study everything.

I hadn't slept a wink all night. Instead, I'd cased the grounds, measured distances, and planned attack methods and escape routes—anything to keep my mind off the

Sprytes' deadline and everything to ensure no one snuck up on me in the dark.

I'd stayed jazzed through dawn and sunrise, watching the set-up like a vulture, mildly curious about the large and irregularly shaped wedding gifts stacked on top of and around one table. I couldn't see through the wrapping, but I didn't spend much energy trying. The guests, as they trickled in, commanded most of my attention.

Rather than suits or dresses, all were wrapped from head to toe in fashionably arranged scarves featuring a variety of patterns—combinations of black, white, and gray. Only their eyes, their manicured hands, and their stylish shoes were visible. I made a few reasonable guesses, but it was near impossible to tell who was a man and who was a woman. None wore heels or loafers or any other footwear that leaned toward one gender; unisex platform shoes or boots all around. I'd tried x-raying in the area of the chest and crotches of a few, but much like the gifts' wrapping paper, something about the composition of the fabric prevented me from seeing through.

Was mummy chic the latest fashion for weddings? Or was this couple just ahead of the curve? Regardless, the colors and styles seemed more appropriate for a bizarre funeral than a fun wedding. Maybe the HSA agent was more of a twisted sicko than Bruce's intel had let on.

Speak of the devil...

The groom exited from one of the former barns and sauntered toward the gathering, walking quite properly in straight lines and making right-angle turns. A slender man wearing some kind of full-body black suit that covered everything but his eyes, mouth, and maybe nostrils. It wasn't quite skin-tight, but the outfit was close-fitting enough to dispel any questions about gender. What was it? Leather?

Spandex? Rubber? Of course my sight couldn't penetrate the material—but I was sure one of my blades could.

And here was the bride, all decked out in white. A small, thin girl wearing another full-body suit that only let eyes and mouth greet fresh air.

If nothing else, I admired the wedding planner. After this was over, I'd have to look her up, maybe recruit her and have her design me some new outfits. She and Bruce could be the beginning of me building my own little fashionable team of vigilantes.

The bride and groom took their positions, and the officiant—an oddly proportioned figure wrapped in the most colorful scarves—raised his or her hands majestically, commanding all attention and silencing all tongues. Even when this master or mistress of ceremonies began to speak, its gender was not apparent. *No matter.* That fool wasn't a target.

I manipulated the light around my body—transitioning from camo to invisibility—as I levitated down from my branch. I took care that my footfalls were softer than a cat's as I crisscrossed through the rows of vines and made my way to the house. It took no great effort to scale the side. From the roof, I could easily jump and glide, felling the groom with one swipe, if not decapitating him outright. I'd resolved to do it right after he and the bride kissed, when they'd undoubtedly have to pull off those ridiculous masks.

I was tense. *Ready.* Then the preacher called for the ring.

There was no best man. There were six pallbearers.

Enwrapped in black scarves, they exited one of the buildings and walked a dividing line between the guests toward the bride and groom. They carried a crystal coffin. A sleeping teenage girl lay inside. A chubby redhead—naked, bruised, blemished, freckled, and scarred. Some of her wounds had healed badly; others seemed freshly made, suppurating, slowly healing, scabbing over...

What the hell was all this?

Bruce had mentioned the HSA agent had wanted to buy a redheaded girl. Was this her? Was this wedding-funeral also some sort of auction?

Whatever—the idea behind it all was clearly disgusting. It was time to inject a dose of beautiful chaos.

Still invisible, I leapt and glided at a strategic angle with a double-edged blade in both hands. I was seconds away from cutting away the groom's mask with one and slitting his throat with the other.

The officiant raised his or her hands erratically as something enwrapped and wringed my wrists, forcing me to release my grip, before jerking my entire body off course. I crashed into the gift table.

Stunned, I relinquished my invisibility as I tried to stand.

I couldn't.

I couldn't get to my feet.

The blow hadn't been that hard; I'd suffered worse. The trestle table hadn't even cracked. Neither had any of my bones. The problem was the gifts—their *ribbons*. Some of them had untied from their packages and tied themselves around my arms and legs. They felt like silk against my skin until I shifted or tried to move; then they felt as strong and as sharp as steel. The harder I tried to free myself, the tighter they felt, the *deeper* they cut.

I was now a gift, and I immediately knew for whom.

The officiant, the bride, and the groom loomed over me.

The bride was first. She put her fingers to her neck, parted the seams, and pulled her mask off.

The girl... that *damned* girl from the tea house.

The groom was next. At this point, it shouldn't have been as much of a shock as my voice made it seem, but since my body was trapped, my emotions were getting away from me.

"*Bruce*? What—? You—You, *shit*! What the fuck are you doing?"

He sighed. "I'm sorry, Bet. But they... they..."

"We met up with him during your escapade yesterday," the college girl said. "We made a deal, and we kept our eyes on him to make sure he kept it."

"What *deal*?" I threw the question at Bruce.

"Delivering you to me," the officiant said. "*Alive*. At least, for the moment."

I knew the voice, knew it all too well. It had sounded deeper when she was conducting—or *pretending* to conduct—the ceremony. But now the witch sounded like her regular old ugly self.

She unwrapped the scarves that covered her hair and much of her face. I sat bound, trapped, looking up at the girl whose skin tone gave the impression of a corroded penny.

"You went through a lot of trouble," I said. "Are you that desperate, that *scared* of losing something that doesn't belong to you?"

"No trouble at all," Carmilla said. "Everything important involves ritual and ceremony. And all my Sprytes are valuable, too valuable to be loose, floating purposeless in this world."

"*Witch*, do you have any idea what I've been doing? You should have put your resources at work to help me."

"I know exactly what you've been doing. From day one. I let you go on your merry way until it was necessary to call you back. Now, I've *called*."

"Appearances are deceptive, witch. You still don't have me. You'll *never* have me."

Carmilla smiled and lowered her face closer to mine. " 'Betty,' is it?" She shook her head and *tsked*. "Really poor choice of a nom de plume. You're up against a goddess of gambling, you know. I've yet to lose a bet."

"Maybe," I said. "But all the women you've tricked and kept under your control have lost plenty."

"You mean their names in exchange for wine from the Vine of Life?"

"I mean giving away their bodies, minds, and souls in exchange for a deranged madwoman's bid for Godhood."

Carmilla shrugged as she straightened. "The clothing of thin skins, rotting flesh, and limited minds won't withstand the environment of the new universe."

"And free will? What about that?"

She laughed without making a detectible sound. "I guaranteed you eternal life, *Bet*. But now... Now you want to die having accomplished nothing meaningful."

"I've killed pimps, child enslavers, molesters—some of the ugliest creatures on the planet."

"Uglier ones are coming," Carmilla said. "You were re-made to serve one purpose. The Sprytes have one lofty duty: To help save a *beautiful* child."

The pallbearers brought the crystal coffin into view. I hated, hated, *hated* myself for thinking it—but the girl inside was in no way pretty, never mind beautiful.

"It's really simple," Carmilla said. "We help save this girl, she in turn helps save the chosen for the Hereafter. As I've tried to teach you, The End is very, very near."

I struggled again with the ribbons and bled for it. The Carmilla I knew was not this talented, nowhere near this powerful. Something had happened since I'd left her fold, maybe something that had to do with this redhead, or maybe some of these nameless, faceless *things* around me.

They may've been exercising some sort of influence over the environment. That had to be it. I understood the manipulation of light, not the manipulation of fabric, nor other manipulations... I cast a glance at Bruce, who may as well have been a statue.

"The shadow government," I said, refocusing on the witch. "You're involved somehow. *Why*?"

She smirked. "All governments, whether in shadow or light, will fall. They are of no consequence. My involvement with them or lack thereof is of no consequence. I simply make deals, temporary arrangements with whomever I need to achieve the ultimate. And you"—she nodded at me—"I'm giving you a choice. An ultimate choice. You can decide whether you want to be of any consequence."

"Really?" I tried my best to smirk back at her. "Do you really need me?"

"Despite your transgressions, I'm willing to welcome you back, with no hard feelings."

I struggled with the steel ribbons, again drawing blood.

"But I can't just give you a written test," Carmilla said. "Or an oral one. Poor student that you were, you'd undoubtedly fail. And I want to give you a *fighting* chance."

The ribbons around my arms and legs loosened as some anonymous wedding guests pushed forward two packages, both more than eight feet tall with silver wrapping and golden bows.

I stood, although I didn't know whether it was by my own willpower or that of Carmilla's. She stepped backward, beckoning me forward with her index fingers. I wasn't sure of myself. And I wasn't sure whether the guests had unwrapped the packages or if they had swung open on their own to reveal two tall, fashionable figures: A blonde and a raven-haired brunette, both adorned in war-dresses much prettier than mine.

The blonde predominated in red while the brunette favored blue. They had belts, but no weapons were attached. They stepped out of the boxes like dolls come to life and flanked Carmilla. I had a fleeting impression of the two being Carmilla's accessories. They were the blades in the witch's belt.

"Bet," Carmilla said, "I like to introduce you to Blink"—she pointed a thumb at the blonde, then the brunette—"and Blank. I refer to them and some of the other ladies you've met recently as Killer B's." She laughed another silent laugh, quite appropriate for a humorless joke.

These two were like the women I'd met yesterday, but there was something more to them. Tresses of the blonde's hair obscured her right eye, and the brunette's eyes were so deep in shadow, even out in the midday sunlight, that I couldn't even determine the color of her irises.

When facing off against another Virus-carrier, it was more important to be aware of an opponent's eyes rather than the hands or feet. As I tried to study the eyes of the two ladies, the blonde smiled, and the brunette frowned.

I grimaced. I hadn't come here expecting a real fight. I'd already spent so much energy staying in hiding and sneaking up on a false target. Even at full strength, I wasn't sure I could engage these two and win. But there was no other way out, no way to escape without shedding even more blood.

I dove for blondie, who seemed the softer of the two.

She twirled and dipped, as if led by an unseen dancing partner—but she was in control enough to grab my ankle as I passed.

Blink flung me toward her very visible partner—Blank —who kicked me in the neck. Her foot felt like a brick of ice.

Down on my hands and knees, I was surprised my neck wasn't broken as I turned my head to see blondie's blurred foot nearing my face.

I flattened and rolled away from the reach of both women before scrambling to my feet and dashing for the gift table.

I went for the smaller packages, tossing them, enfolding them in waves of light, making them appear as fiery, flying demons.

It was such an automatic attack method for me that I didn't pause to consider how it might work on those who were equally talented or even more talented.

Blink and Blank dodged and twirled, again as if dancing, moving closer all the while, until they were close enough to dart in on me with sweeping motions.

One went high, the other low. I hopped and bent backward, flattening myself on the table as one of them smoothly ducked under it while the other glided over me.

It was funny how many thoughts a person can have in a split second; they really do slice by at light speed. I congratulated myself on the quick maneuvering and mentally laughed when they failed to connect while at the same time wondering what really made these two living dolls so special as I—

Hands clasped my wrists and ankles.

From beneath the table, Blink had my feet. At my head, Blank held my wrists. Together they pulled, stretching me.

My bones popped, even—*especially*—in parts where there were no joints. The women were doing more than just pulling; they were running a current through me. It was the opposite of a massage. I could imagine-hear-*feel* hairline fractures forming in my bones throughout my body. They were going to break me and rip me wide open.

I looked toward the sky, squinted, and concentrated like a desperate worshipper of Ra.

My skin tightened. My muscles tensed. I ran some currents of my own.

I felt my nerves snap and crackle just a few decibels lower than the shrieks both ladies made when they let me go.

I rolled off the table and quickly scanned my surroundings for the least-resistant path for escaping. The guests were most sparsely clustered at ten o' clock; that's where I darted.

As I neared bodies, I shouted rhythmically, like a cheerleader, trying to encourage the people to move their damn selves out of my way. But they didn't hear me. *I* didn't hear me. My voice box may as well have been an icebox, my tongue a tiny frozen waterfall.

Fuck it—I was prepared to barrel on through the crowd of would-be mummies. A block of ice at the back my knee made me tumble instead.

Blank had caught up and landed a well-placed kick. To replace the shout of pain that somehow wouldn't come, I kicked at her knee in turn. She *blanked* out before I could connect, and the other one *blinked* into sight at my right to kick me in the side of my head.

I rolled with it. Dizzy, I managed to get to my feet. I lunged in the direction of the blonde, only to see her pop out of sight and feel the other one pop in behind me when she kicked me in the lower back.

I wouldn't go down again—I *couldn't*.

I did my best to keep my balance while turning and swinging. Of course she was gone, and I fell to the ground.

But maybe luck—some *beautiful* luck—was on my side. I saw one of my blades within reach. I stretched and grasped it. It was like having an appendage reattached, an appendage that worked effectively and instinctively.

I stood again, if not steadily then at least sure enough to keep my face far away from the ground as I maneuvered, slashing and slicing at everything near me. But the two nearest me were Blink and Blank, who kept blanking out and blinking into sight before I could so much as cut a thread from their clothing, let alone penetrate a layer of skin.

Then one of them appeared inches in front of me, her right hand in an ice-cold vice grip around my throat.

Raven hair—*Blank*. Even at this close range, I could barely make out her irises.

It was then that I realized she and her partner, their names, their methods, and their appearances were all part of some ritual, a very poetic ritual well beyond my understanding.

Everything is ritual... ceremony...

She smiled as if reading my thought. I made a move to plunge my knife into her abdomen. She opened her mouth and *hissed*, spraying a cold perfumed mist all over my face before letting me go.

The fragrant spittle warmed quickly and burned like acid, washing away my makeup, letting the sun play havoc with my face, and distorting my senses of sight and sound.

As I stumbled, trying to fight back against the loss of direction, the loss of my place in this wide chaos, the ceremony progressed as the surrounding crowd sang a song. To my ears it sounded like a turgid dirge that made numerous connections between love and blood, marriage and war. They sang as they moved, keeping me and my two *elusives* forever encircled. And from somewhere both beyond and amid it all, I heard Carmilla, taunting me with crystal-clear words as Blink and Blank assaulted me with hands and feet I couldn't see coming.

"Your tricks are corrupt. *Rough*. Not sublime. Not beautiful. *Ugly*—like you. You truly don't know what you're doing, or why."

The witch was right. I couldn't win. I couldn't escape. I couldn't even speak. I just continued to move, twirling, whirling, sweeping, and windmilling my arms in attempts to smack, slap, cut, and chop my two enemies, my two dancing partners... partners who cut up my dress, slapped away the tatters, and chipped away at my makeup, my skin, my flesh...

They wouldn't take my mind. They *couldn't*.

But they had drawn me into a pattern, and my movements were just giving it further details. I was losing it—my body, my consciousness...

My last coherent thought was of Bruce, my trusted valet. Yesterday, he'd procured the medications I'd taken this morning. There was no question about from whom he'd really gotten them. There was no question that I couldn't trust anyone any more. Now, all was Blink and Blank—kicks, punches, and tosses—until it all went *black*.

MY EYES WERE OPENED by a song.

This one was joyous, far more cheerful than the one that had accompanied my thrashing. It had the tone and words of a true wedding song; the refrain was "Always." The same crowd of enwrapped wedding guests sang it. They were fanned out before me, like tangible spirits, solidified ghosts.

And I again was entangled, this time in vines, hanging from a trellis at the edge of the vineyard.

Carmilla, Blink, and Blank stood mere feet in front of me. Each held one hand behind their backs and the other upraised, grasping a crystal goblet half full of what appeared to be white wine.

"Congratulations," the witch said. "I've decided to welcome you back."

The three of them clinked then sipped from their glasses.

"Wh-What..." My larynx and tongue were as unsteady as my eyelids. "What... what is all this? What's happening?"

"Reparation," Carmilla said. "You were a wreck before I found you and tried to repair you, beautify you. But you got lost, and I found you again—"

Something quickened within me, sharpening my senses and my tongue.

"Li-like a rusty instrument," I said, "or a broken robot... That's how you see women, *all* women who aren't under your complete control. You were never any better than the pimps I've executed. All you want is pretty, plastic-skinned tools, all of them working to create something they'll never truly share."

What I'd said had been honest from the heart, but the words weren't completely mine, nor was the energy that spurred the outburst. I cast a glance to my left and spotted the crystal coffin and the comatose girl inside. Was she— that *ugly* girl—reaching out through me? Using me to cry for help?

Whatever the explanation, there was nothing I could do about it; the green vines entangling me seemed stronger than steel. And for her part, Carmilla was oblivious to any connection between me and the girl. The witch kept her eyes on me as she spoke.

"You keep trying to break free," she said, "but you have always been nothing more than a damaged doll, a puppet with limp limbs and fraying strings, not fit to be released from her packaging yet. You had a philosophy, but it didn't make complete sense. You had a course of action, but the path was too dark and had no end in sight. I tried to teach you the underlying lessons of New Creation, but you saw flaws." She chuckled. "Sister, there was *never* any flaw in my magick; there were only flaws in your being. But you have wisdom enough to understand that you can't be allowed to exist. It's necessary for me to kill my *ugliest* creations."

She and her companions revealed their hidden hands; each held a long blade. Blink and Blank clutched those I'd brought with me. Carmilla's, with its jewel-encrusted hilt, was clearly ceremonial but no less sharp.

I had no words. And even if she had inspired me before, the girl in the casket was now as lifeless as she looked. All of my hope lay in the coffin with her.

This, *all* of this, wasn't just the gathering of a lost soul. This had been a demonstration for the guests—the nameless and faceless of Carmilla's nextworld government, bidden to sing without understanding the words. They were witnessing what happened to traitors because there was so much at stake in the grotesque game of war that Carmilla was playing.

"Beauty has been cheapened in our society," the witch said. "And so has death. But don't worry. I'll make yours mean something."

Carmilla zipped her blade across my throat; Blink and Blank mimicked in rapid succession. In unison, they raised their glasses. I forced my eyes to stay open as I felt my last breaths leave me. I could only maintain long enough to see the three swirl their glasses, hold them up to the sunlight, then take generous sips.

The only words I heard before my senses blurred were "Welcome back into the fold."

ABOUT THE SERIES

Eve of Light is a Dark Metaphysical Fantasy series chronicling the surreal events leading up to the Apocalypse—the Death of God. The setting is a contemporary, alternate Earth on the verge of a cataclysm that will warp space, time, and minds. The main narrative of those plotting and battling to save humanity is told in the *Eve of Light* series of novels. The short stories and novellas are simply flashes on the fringe—episodes told from the perspective of everyday men and women living in a world turned weird.

The Core Novels
BloodLight: The Apocalypse of Robert Goldner
Broken Angels *(Eve of Light * Book I)*
Divinities, Entangled *(Eve of Light * Book II)*

Stories on the Fringe
FoolKillers
The Lark
Heaven's Gun
Knotty & Ice
Rogue Beauty
Deviant-Hunter's Sabbath

ABOUT THE AUTHOR

Harambee K. Grey-Sun writes under the broad umbrella of speculative fiction. He integrates elements of fantasy, horror, noir, black humor, and science fiction into his work and spins dark, surreal, mysterious, grotesque, at times challenging, and often blasphemous tales. Many of his stories can be categorized into one or more of the following subgenres: speculative thriller, urban fantasy, metaphysical fantasy, superhero, occult/supernatural, slipstream, and–*of course*– weird fiction. His Dark Metaphysical Fantasy series *Eve of Light* examines the dark nature of God and what it really means to be human.

For more information:
www.harambeegreysun.com